W9-BLL-736

Quentin Blake
Loveykins

PEACHTREE
ATLANTA

Angela Bowling took her shopping bag and set off for the village. It was a bright spring morning, but the wind had blown all night in the great woods and there were leaves and fallen branches everywhere.

And there was something else . . .

"My goodness," said Angela. "It's a baby bird blown out of his nest. This little loveykins needs someone to look after him."

She wrapped him up carefully in her scarf,
and took him home with her.

When they got there Angela added a shawl and an old sweater so that the little bird would be warm and safe. Then she sat him in a lovely basket that once used to hold flowers.

She fed him with spoonfuls of warm milk.

"He should have a name," said Angela.
"I shall call him Augustus."

Only the best was good enough for Augustus.

Angela fed the baby bird creamed carrots,

chocolate éclairs,

Black Forest cake,

and boxes of chocolates with assorted fillings.

Augustus ate the whole box.

"Who's a loveykins, then?" said Angela.

The next morning Angela bought a fancy new stroller. It had a special umbrella to keep off the rain and the sun.

Every morning after that Angela would wrap Augustus up carefully so that he didn't catch cold, and they would set off to the village.

They met Elsie Lyons and the twins by
the duck pond . . .

Miss Twyford and her dollies
on High Street . . .

and Harold and his brother Gerald with
their dog Wellington outside the library.

At the village store Angela Bowling bought
all the best things to eat that she could find.

Augustus ate and ate, and as the days went by he grew bigger and bigger.

At last he was too big for his basket, and too big for the stroller, especially with all those sweaters and blankets wrapped round him to make sure he didn't catch cold.

So Angela Bowling bought a brand-new
garden shed especially for Augustus.
Every morning she would take him a tray
of good things to eat.

And then once again there came a night
of dreadful weather, and big winds blew
through the great woods.

In the morning Angela Bowling got up, put
on her robe, and stepped out to see
how her little loveykins had spent the night.

But what did she see before her?

The garden shed had been blown flat by
the wind, and there, with piles of blankets and
sweaters strewn about him, stood
Augustus, shaking his wings.

Angela Bowling
fainted clean away.

Augustus covered her
carefully with a pink
flowery blanket.

Then, with his wings creaking slightly from lack of use, he began to fly.

He flew through the village, over
Elsie Lyons and the twins . . .

over Miss Twyford and
her dollies . . .

and over Harold and his
brother Gerald and
their dog Wellington.

He flew up into the trees of the great woods.
There he ate several beetles and the remains
of a dead squirrel.

And then he flew on up,
up into the bright blue sky.

Further and further he rose, circling on the warm winds high above the clouds.

Far below he could see Angela Bowling
sleeping peacefully under the pink flowery
blanket, and stretched out before him—

Such prospects!

Such vistas!

It took Angela Bowling a long time to recover from her shock, but after six months she had her garden shed rebuilt. In it she started a wonderful collection of cactuses of all shapes and sizes.

And every so often, just when she is least expecting it, there is a rustle of wings and Augustus is there on the roof of the shed. He always brings Angela a present: a dead mouse, perhaps, or a few beetles.

She never eats them.

Published by
PEACHTREE PUBLISHERS, LTD.
1700 Chattahoochee Avenue
Atlanta, Georgia 30318-2112

www.peachtree-online.com

First published in Great Britain in 2002 by Random House Children's Books.

Printed in Singapore by Tien Wah Press

10 9 8 7 6 5 4 3 2 1
First Edition

Cataloging-in-Publication Data is available from the Library of Congress